Cinderella
and Other Stories from "The Blue Fairy Book"

Unabridged

ANDREW LANG

Illustrated by Marty Noble

DOVER PUBLICATIONS, INC.
Mineola, New York

DOVER CHILDREN'S THRIFT CLASSICS
EDITOR OF THIS VOLUME: CANDACE WARD

Copyright

Published in Canada by General Publishing Company, Ltd., 30 Lesmill Road, Don Mills, Toronto, Ontario.

Bibliographical Note

This Dover edition, first published in 1996, is a new selection of six stories adapted from *The Blue Fairy Book* (New York: Dover Publications, Inc., 1965), edited by Andrew Lang and first published by Longmans, Green, and Co., London, in 1889. The interior illustrations, by Marty Noble; the cover illustration, by Thea Kliros; and the introductory Note have been prepared specially for this edition.

Library of Congress Cataloging-in-Publication Data

Cinderella and other stories from The blue fairy book / Andrew Lang, [editor] ; illustrated by Marty Noble.
    p.   cm. — (Dover children's thrift classics)
    Contents: Cinderella — The bronze ring — Felicia and the pot of pinks — The white cat — The story of pretty Goldilocks — Snow White and Rose Red.
    ISBN 0-486-29389-0
    1. Fairy tales. [1. Fairy tales. 2. Folklore.] I. Lang, Andrew, 1844–1912. II. Noble, Marty, 1948– ill. III. Cinderella. English. IV. Series.
PZ8.C495   1996
[398.2]—dc20   96-9803
                                               CIP
                                               AC

Manufactured in the United States of America
Dover Publications, Inc., 31 East 2nd Street, Mineola, N.Y. 11501

Note

In the late nineteenth century the Scottish folklorist Andrew Lang published a number of fairy-tale collections for children in volumes named after different colors. The stories in the present Dover book have all been taken, with adaptations, from *The Blue Fairy Book*.

"Cinderella," the most famous of these stories, is based on the French version by Charles Perrault, not the German version by the Grimm Brothers. "The Bronze Ring" is from Turkey. "Felicia and the Pot of Pinks," "The White Cat" and "The Story of Pretty Goldilocks" (not connected with "The Three Bears") are French stories by the Countess d'Aulnoy. "Snow-white and Rose-red" is by the Grimm Brothers.

Contents

Cinderella

ONCE THERE WAS a gentleman who married, for his second wife, the proudest and most haughty woman that was ever seen. She had, by a former husband, two daughters of similar nature, who were, indeed, exactly like her in all things. He had likewise, by another wife, a young daughter, but of great goodness and sweetness of temper, which she took from her mother, who had been the best creature in the world.

No sooner were the ceremonies of the wedding over than the stepmother began to show herself in her true colors. She could not bear the good qualities of this pretty girl, especially since they made her own daughters appear the more hateful. She employed her in the meanest work of the house: she scoured the dishes, tables, etc., and scrubbed madam's chamber, and those of her daughters; she slept up in a sorry garret, upon a wretched straw bed, while her sisters had fine rooms and slept upon beds of the very newest fashion, and had looking-glasses so large that they might see themselves from head to foot.

The poor girl bore all patiently, and dared not tell her father, for his wife governed him entirely. When she

1

Her godmother asked what was the matter.

had done her work, she used to go into the chimney-corner, and sit down among cinders and ashes, which made her commonly be called *Cinderwench;* but the youngest stepsister, who was not so rude and uncivil as the eldest, called her Cinderella. However, Cinderella, notwithstanding her ragged clothes, was a hundred times handsomer than her sisters, though they were always dressed very richly.

It happened that the King's son gave a ball, and invited all the people of fashion to it. Cinderella's sisters were also invited, for they cut a very grand figure among the quality. They were mightily delighted at this invitation, and wonderfully busy in choosing out their most becoming gowns, petticoats, and head-dresses. This was a new trouble to Cinderella; for it was she who ironed her sisters' linen, and sewed their ruffles; they talked all day long of nothing but how they should be dressed.

"For my part," said the eldest, "I will wear my red velvet suit with French trimming."

"And I," said the youngest, "shall have my usual petticoat; but I will put on my gold-flowered cloak, and my diamond belt, which is far from being the most ordinary one in the world."

They sent for the best hair-dresser they could get, and Cinderella was also called up to be consulted in all these matters, for she had excellent notions, and advised them always for the best, and even offered her services to dress their hair, which they were very willing she should do. As she was doing this, they said to her:

"Cinderella, wouldn't you be glad to go to the ball?"

"Alas!" said she, "you only tease me; a servant-girl like me could not go."

"You are right," they replied; "it would make the people laugh to see a Cinderwench at a ball."

Anyone but Cinderella would have dressed their hair badly, but she was very good, and dressed them perfectly well. They were almost two days without eating, so much they were transported with joy. They broke dozens of laces trying to be laced up tight, that they might have a fine slender shape, and they were continually at their looking-glass. At last the happy day came; they went to Court, and Cinderella followed them with her eyes as long as she could, and when she had lost sight of them, she fell a-crying.

Her godmother, who saw her all in tears, asked her what was the matter.

"I wish I could—I wish I could—"; she was not able to speak the rest, being interrupted by her tears and sobbing.

The pumpkin was turned into a fine coach.

This godmother of hers, who was a fairy, said to her, "You wish you could go to the ball; is it not so?"

"Y—es," cried Cinderella, with a great sigh.

"Well," said her godmother, "be but a good girl, and I will arrange everything." Then she took her into her chamber, and said to her, "Run into the garden, and bring me a pumpkin."

Cinderella went immediately to gather the finest she could get, and brought it to her godmother, not being able to imagine how this pumpkin could make her go to the ball. Her godmother scooped out all the inside of it, leaving nothing but the rind; which done, she struck it with her wand, and the pumpkin was instantly turned into a fine coach, gilded all over with gold.

She then went to look into her mouse-trap, where she found six mice, all alive, and ordered Cinderella to lift up a little the trap-door, when, giving each mouse, as it went out, a little tap with her wand, the mouse was that moment turned into a fine horse, which altogether made a very fine set of six horses of a beautiful mouse-colored dapple-grey.

Observing that there was no coachman, Cinderella said, "I will go and see if there is a rat in the rat-trap—we may make a coachman of him."

"You are right," replied her godmother; "go and look."

Cinderella brought the trap to her, and in it there were three huge rats. The fairy chose the one which had the largest beard, and, having touched him with her wand, he was turned into a fat, jolly coachman, who had the smartest whiskers eyes ever beheld. After that, she said to her:

"Go again into the garden, and you will find six lizards behind the watering-pot; bring them to me."

She had no sooner done so than her godmother turned them into six footmen, who skipped up immediately behind the coach, with their liveries all covered with gold and silver, and clung as close behind each other as if they had done nothing else their whole lives. The Fairy then said to Cinderella:

"Well, you see here a coach fit to go to the ball in; are you not pleased with it?"

"Oh! yes," cried she; "but must I go there as I am, in these nasty rags?"

Her godmother only just touched her with her wand, and, at the same instant, her clothes were turned into cloth of gold and silver, all beset with jewels. This done, she gave her a pair of glass slippers, the prettiest in the whole world. As she got up into her coach, her godmother commanded her not to stay till after midnight, telling her that if she stayed one moment longer, the coach would be a pumpkin again, her horses mice, her coachman a rat, her footmen lizards, and her clothes become just as they were before.

She promised her godmother she would not fail to leave the ball before midnight; and then away she went, scarce able to contain herself for joy. The King's son, who was told that a great princess, whom nobody knew, had arrived, ran out to receive her; he gave her his hand as she alighted out of the coach, and led her into the hall, among all the company. There was immediately a profound silence, they stopped dancing, and the violins ceased to play, so attentive was everyone to contemplate the singular beauties of the unknown newcomer. Nothing was then heard but a confused noise of:

"Ha! how handsome she is! Ha! how handsome she is!"

The King himself, old as he was, could not help watching her, and told the Queen softly that it was a long time since he had seen so beautiful and lovely a creature.

All the ladies were busied in considering her clothes and head-dress, that they might have some made next day after the same pattern, provided they could find such fine materials and as able hands to make them.

The King's son conducted her to the most honorable seat, and afterwards took her out to dance with him; she danced so very gracefully that they all admired her more and more. A fine dinner was served up, but the young Prince ate not a morsel, so intently was he gazing at her.

She went and sat down by her sisters, showing them a thousand civilities, giving them part of the oranges and citrons which the Prince had presented her with, which very much surprised them, for they did not recognize her. While Cinderella was thus amusing her sisters, she heard the clock strike eleven and three-quar-

The King's son took her out to dance with him.

ters, whereupon she immediately made a courtesy to the company and hasted away as fast as she could.

When she got home, she ran to find her godmother, and, after thanking her, she said she could not help wishing she might go next day to the ball, because the King's son had invited her.

As she was eagerly telling her godmother what had passed at the ball, her two sisters knocked at the door, which Cinderella ran and opened.

"How long you have stayed!" cried she, yawning, rubbing her eyes and stretching herself as if she had been just waked out of her sleep.

"If you had been at the ball," says one of her sisters, "you would not be tired. There was the finest princess, the most beautiful ever was seen with mortal eyes; she showed us a thousand civilities, and gave us oranges and citrons."

Cinderella seemed very indifferent in the matter; indeed, she asked them the name of that princess; but they told her they did not know it, and that the King's son was very curious about her and would give all the world to know who she was. At this Cinderella, smiling, replied:

"She must, then, be very beautiful indeed; how happy you have been! Could not I see her? Ah! dear Miss Charlotte, do lend me your yellow dress which you wear every day."

"Ay, to be sure!" cried Miss Charlotte; "lend my clothes to such a dirty Cinderwench as you are! I would be a fool."

Cinderella, indeed, expected such an answer, and was very glad of the refusal; for she would have been sadly put to it if her sister had lent her what she asked for jestingly.

When the clock struck twelve, she rose up and fled.

The next day the two sisters were at the ball, and so was Cinderella, but dressed more magnificently than before. The King's son was always by her, and never ceased his compliments and kind speeches to her; Cinderella was so pleased with his attentions that she quite forgot her godmother's warning, so that when the clock struck twelve, she at first took it to be no more than eleven; she then rose up and fled, as nimble as a deer. The Prince followed, but could not overtake her. She left behind one of her glass slippers, which the Prince took up most carefully. She got home, but quite out of breath, and in her nasty old clothes, having nothing left of all her finery but one of the little slippers, fellow to that she dropped. The guards at the palace gate were asked:

If they had seen a princess go out.

Who said: They had seen nobody go out but a young girl, very poorly dressed, and who looked more like a poor country wench than a gentlewoman.

When the two sisters returned from the ball Cinderella asked them if they had been well entertained, and if the fine lady had been there.

They told her yes, but that she hurried away immediately when it struck twelve, and with so much haste that she dropped one of her little glass slippers, the prettiest in the world, which the King's son had picked up; that he had done nothing but look at her all the time at the ball, and that most certainly he was very much in love with the beautiful person who owned the glass slipper.

What they said was very true; for a few days later the King's son ordered a proclamation that he would marry her whose foot this slipper would just fit. His ambassadors began to try it upon the princesses, then the duchesses and all the ladies of the Court, but in vain; it was brought to the two sisters, who did all they possibly could to thrust their foot into the slipper, but they could not do it. Cinderella, who saw all this, and knew her slipper, said to them, laughing:

"Let me see if it will fit me."

Her sisters burst out laughing, and began to tease her. The gentleman who was sent to try the slipper looked earnestly at Cinderella, and, finding her very handsome, said:

It was but just that she should try, and that he had orders to let everyone make trial.

He obliged Cinderella to sit down, and, putting the slipper to her foot, he found it went on very easily, and fitted her as if had been made of wax. The astonishment her two sisters were in was excessively great, but still abundantly greater when Cinderella pulled out of her pocket the other slipper, and put it on her foot. Thereupon, in came her godmother, who, having touched with her wand Cinderella's clothes, made them richer and more magnificent than any of those she had before.

And now her two sisters found her to be that fine, beautiful lady whom they had seen at the ball. They threw themselves at her feet to beg pardon for all the ill-treatment they had made her undergo. Cinderella took them up, and, as she embraced them, cried:

That she forgave them with all her heart, and desired them always to love her.

She was conducted to the young Prince, dressed as she was; he thought her more charming than ever, and, a few days after, married her. Cinderella, who was no less good than beautiful, gave her two sisters lodgings in the palace, and that very same day married them to two great lords of the Court.

The Bronze Ring

ONCE UPON A TIME in a certain country there lived a king whose palace was surrounded by a spacious garden. But, though the gardeners were many and the soil was good, this garden yielded neither flowers nor fruits, not even grass or shady trees.

The King was in despair about it when a wise old man said to him:

"Your gardeners do not understand their business: but what can you expect of men whose fathers were cobblers and carpenters? How should they have learnt to cultivate your garden?"

"You are quite right," cried the King.

"Therefore," continued the old man, "you should send for a gardener whose father and grandfather have been gardeners before him, and very soon your garden will be full of green grass and gay flowers, and you will enjoy its delicious fruit."

So the King sent messengers to every town, village, and hamlet in his dominions, to look for a gardener whose forefathers had been gardeners also, and after forty days one was found.

"Come with us and be gardener to the King," they said to him.

"How can I go to the King," said the gardener, "a poor wretch like me?"

"That is of no consequence," they answered. "Here are new clothes for you and your family."

"But I owe money to several people."

"We will pay your debts," they said.

So the gardener allowed himself to be persuaded, and went away with the messengers, taking his wife and his son with him; and the King, delighted to have found a real gardener, entrusted him with the care of his garden. The man found no difficulty in making the royal garden produce flowers and fruit, and at the end of a year the park was not like the same place, and the King showered gifts upon his new servant.

The gardener, as you have heard already, had a son, who was a very handsome young man, with most agreeable manners, and every day he carried the best fruit of the garden to the King, and all the prettiest flowers to his daughter. Now this princess was wonderfully pretty and was just sixteen years old, and the King was beginning to think it was time that she should be married.

"My dear child," said he, "you are of an age to take a husband, therefore I am thinking of marrying you to the son of my prime minister."

"Father," replied the Princess, "I will never marry the son of the minister."

"Why not?" asked the King.

"Because I love the gardener's son," answered the Princess.

On hearing this the King was at first very angry, and then he wept and sighed, and declared that such a husband was not worthy of his daughter; but the young

Princess was not to be turned from her resolution to marry the gardener's son.

Then the King consulted his ministers. "This is what you must do," they said. "To get rid of the gardener you must send both suitors to a very distant country, and the one who returns first shall marry your daughter."

The King followed this advice, and the minister's son was presented with a splendid horse and a purse full of gold pieces, while the gardener's son had only an old lame horse and a purse full of copper money, and every one thought he would never come back from his journey.

The day before they started the Princess met her lover and said to him:

"Be brave, and remember always that I love you. Take this purse full of jewels and make the best use you can of them for love of me, and come back quickly and demand my hand."

The two suitors left the town together, but the minister's son went off at a gallop on his good horse, and very soon was lost to sight behind the most distant hills. He travelled on for some days, and presently reached a fountain beside which an old woman all in rags sat upon a stone.

"Good-day to you, young traveller," said she.

But the minister's son made no reply.

"Have pity upon me, traveller," she said again. "I am dying of hunger, as you see, and three days have I been here and no one has given me anything."

"Let me alone, old witch," cried the young man; "I can do nothing for you," and so saying he went on his way.

That same evening the gardener's son rode up to the fountain upon his lame grey horse.

"Good-day to you, young traveller," said the beggar-woman.

"Good-day, good woman," answered he.

"Young traveller, have pity upon me."

"Take my purse, good woman," said he, "and mount behind me, for your legs can't be very strong."

The old woman didn't wait to be asked twice, but mounted behind him, and in this style they reached the chief city of a powerful kingdom. The minister's son was lodged in a grand inn, the gardener's son and the old woman dismounted at the inn for beggars.

The next day the gardener's son heard a great noise in the street, and the King's heralds passed, blowing all kinds of instruments, and crying:

"The King, our master, is old and infirm. He will give a great reward to whoever will cure him and give him back the strength of his youth."

Then the old beggar-woman said to her benefactor:

"This is what you must do to obtain the reward which the King promises. Go out of the town by the south gate, and there you will find three little dogs of different colors; the first will be white, the second black, the third red. You must kill them and then burn them separately, and gather up the ashes. Put the ashes of each dog into a bag of its own color, then go before the door of the palace and cry out, 'A celebrated physician has come from Janina in Albania. He alone can cure the King and give him back the strength of his youth.' The King's physicians will say, 'This is an impostor, and not a learned man,' and they will make all sorts of difficulties, but you will overcome them all at last, and will present yourself before the sick King. You must then demand as much wood as three mules can carry, and a great cauldron, and must shut yourself up in a room with the Sultan, and when the cauldron boils you must throw him into it, and there leave him until his flesh is completely separated from his bones. Then

The young man followed the woman's directions.

arrange the bones in their proper places, and throw over them the ashes out of the three bags. The King will come back to life, and will be just as he was when he was twenty years old. For your reward you must demand the bronze ring which has the power to grant you everything you desire. Go, my son, and do not forget any of my instructions."

The young man followed the old beggar-woman's directions. On going out of the town he found the white, red, and black dogs, and killed and burnt them, gathering the ashes into three bags. Then he ran to the palace and cried:

"A celebrated physician has just come from Janina in Albania. He alone can cure the King and give him back the strength of his youth."

Immediately a ship appeared upon the sea.

The King's physicians at first laughed at the unknown wayfarer, but the Sultan ordered that the stranger should be admitted. They brought the cauldron and the loads of wood, and very soon the King was boiling away. Towards mid-day the gardener's son arranged the bones in their places, and he had hardly scattered the ashes over them before the old King revived, to find himself once more young and hearty.

"How can I reward you, my benefactor?" he cried. "Will you take half my treasures?"

"No," said the gardener's son.

"My daughter's hand?"

"No."

"Take half my kingdom."

"No. Give me only the bronze ring which can instantly grant me anything I wish for."

"Alas!" said the King, "I set great store by that marvellous ring; nevertheless, you shall have it." And he gave it to him.

The gardener's son went back to say good-bye to the old beggar-woman; then he said to the bronze ring:

"Prepare a splendid ship in which I may continue my journey. Let the hull be of fine gold, the masts of silver, the sails of brocade; let the crew consist of twelve young men of noble appearance, dressed like kings. St. Nicholas will be at the helm. As to the cargo, let it be diamonds, rubies, emeralds, and carbuncles."

And immediately a ship appeared upon the sea which resembled in every particular the description given by the gardener's son, and, stepping on board, he continued his journey. Presently he arrived at a great town and established himself in a wonderful palace. After several days he met his rival, the minister's son, who had spent all his money and was reduced to the disagreeable employment of a carrier of dust and rubbish. The gardener's son said to him:

"What is your name, what is your family, and from what country do you come?"

"I am the son of the prime minister of a great nation, and yet see what a degrading occupation I am reduced to."

"Listen to me; though I don't know anything more about you, I am willing to help you. I will give you a ship to take you back to your own country upon one condition."

"Whatever it may be, I accept it willingly."

"Follow me to my palace."

The minister's son followed the rich stranger, whom he had not recognised. When they reached the palace the gardener's son made a sign to his slaves, who completely undressed the new-comer.

"Make this ring red hot," commanded the master, "and mark the man with it upon his back."

The slaves obeyed him.

"Now, young man," said the rich stranger, "I am going to give you a vessel which will take you back to your own country."

And, going out, he took the bronze ring and said:

"Bronze ring, obey thy master. Prepare me a ship of which the half-rotten timbers shall be painted black, let the sails be in rags, and the sailors infirm and sickly. One shall have lost a leg, another an arm, the third shall be a hunchback, another lame or club-footed or blind, and most of them shall be ugly and covered with scars. Go, and let my orders be executed."

The minister's son embarked in this old vessel, and, thanks to favorable winds, at length reached his own country. In spite of the pitiable condition in which he returned they received him joyfully.

"I am the first to come back," said he to the King; "now fulfill your promise, and give me the princess in marriage."

So they at once began to prepare for the wedding festivities. As to the poor princess, she was sorrowful and angry enough about it.

The next morning, at daybreak, a wonderful ship with every sail set came to anchor before the town. The King happened at that moment to be at the palace window.

"What strange ship is this," he cried, "that has a golden hull, silver masts, and silken sails, and who are the young men like princes who man it? And do I not see St. Nicholas at the helm? Go at once and invite the captain of the ship to come to the palace."

His servants obeyed him, and very soon in came an enchantingly handsome young prince, dressed in rich silk, ornamented with pearls and diamonds.

"Young man," said the King, "you are welcome, whoever you may be. Do me the favor to be my guest as long as you remain in my capital."

"Many thanks, sire," replied the captain, "I accept your offer."

"My daughter is about to be married," said the King; "will you give her away?"

"I shall be charmed, sire."

Soon after came the Princess and her betrothed.

"Why, how is this?" cried the young captain; "would you marry this charming princess to such a man as that?"

"But he is my prime minister's son!"

"What does that matter? I cannot give your daughter away. The man she is betrothed to is one of my servants."

"Your servant?"

"Without doubt. I met him in a distant town reduced to carrying away dust and rubbish from the houses. I had pity on him and engaged him as one of my servants."

"It is impossible!" cried the King.

"Do you wish me to prove what I say? This young man returned in a vessel which I fitted out for him, an unseaworthy ship with a black battered hull, and the sailors were infirm and crippled."

"It is quite true," said the King.

"It is false," cried the minister's son. "I do not know this man!"

"Sire," said the young captain, "order your daughter's betrothed to be stripped, and see if the mark of my ring is not branded upon his back."

The King was about to give this order, when the minister's son, to save himself from such an indignity, admitted that the story was true.

"And now, sire," said the young captain, "do not you recognise me?"

"I recognise you," said the Princess; "you are the gardener's son whom I have always loved, and it is you I wish to marry."

"Young man, you shall be my son-in-law," cried the King. "The marriage festivities are already begun, so you shall marry my daughter this very day."

And so that very day the gardener's son married the beautiful Princess.

Several months passed. The young couple were as happy as the day was long, and the King was more and more pleased with himself for having secured such a son-in-law.

But, presently, the captain of the golden ship found it necessary to take a long voyage, and after embracing his wife tenderly he embarked.

Now in the outskirts of the capital there lived a man who had spent his life in studying black arts—alchemy, astrology, magic, and enchantment. This man found out that the gardener's son had only succeeded in marrying the Princess by the help of the genii who obeyed the bronze ring.

"I will have that ring," said he to himself. So he went down to the sea-shore and caught some little red fishes. Really, they were quite wonderfully pretty. Then he came back, and, passing before the Princess's window, he began to cry out:

"Who wants some pretty little red fishes?"

The Princess heard him, and sent out one of her slaves, who said to the magician:

"What will you take for your fish?"

"A bronze ring."

"A bronze ring, old simpleton! And where shall I find one?"

"Under the cushion in the Princess's room."

The slave went back to her mistress.

"The old madman will take neither gold nor silver," said she.

"What does he want then?"

"A bronze ring that is hidden under a cushion."

"Find the ring and give it to him," said the Princess.

And at last the slave found the bronze ring, which the captain of the golden ship had accidentally left behind, and carried it to the magician, who made off with it instantly.

Hardly had he reached his own house when, taking the ring, he said, "Bronze ring, obey thy master. I desire that the golden ship shall turn to black wood, and the crew to hideous ogres; that St. Nicholas shall leave the helm, and that the only cargo shall be black cats."

The crew was turned to hideous ogres.

And the genii of the bronze ring obeyed him.

Finding himself upon the sea in this miserable condition, the young captain understood that some one must have stolen the bronze ring from him, and he lamented his misfortune loudly; but that did him no good.

"Alas!" he said to himself, "whoever has taken my ring has probably taken my dear wife also. What good will it do me to go back to my own country?" And he sailed about from island to island, and from shore to shore, believing that wherever he went everybody was laughing at him, and very soon his poverty was so great that he and his crew and the poor black cats had nothing to eat but herbs and roots. After wandering about a long time he reached an island inhabited by mice. The captain landed upon the shore and began to explore the country. There were mice everywhere, and nothing but mice. Some of the black cats had followed him, and, not having been fed for several days, they were fearfully hungry, and made terrible havoc among the mice.

Then the queen of the mice held a council.

"These cats will eat every one of us," she said, "if the captain of the ship does not shut the ferocious animals up. Let us send a deputation to him of the bravest among us."

Several mice offered themselves for this mission and set out to find the young captain.

"Captain," said they, "go away quickly from our island, or we shall perish, every mouse of us."

"Willingly," replied the young captain, "upon one condition. That is that you shall first bring me back a bronze ring which some clever magician has stolen from me. If you do not do this I will land all my cats upon your island, and you shall be exterminated."

The mice withdrew in great dismay. "What is to be done?" said the queen. "How can we find this bronze ring?" She held a new council, calling in mice from every quarter of the globe, but nobody knew where the bronze ring was. Suddenly three mice arrived from a very distant country. One was blind, the second lame, and the third had her ears cropped.

"Ho, ho, ho!" said the new-comers. "We come from a far distant country."

"Do you know where the bronze ring is which the genii obey?"

"Ho, ho, ho! we know; a wicked man has taken possession of it, and now he keeps it in his pocket by day and in his mouth by night."

"Go and take it from him, and come back as soon as possible."

So the three mice made themselves a boat and set sail for the magician's country. When they reached the capital they landed and ran to the palace, leaving only the blind mouse on the shore to take care of the boat. Then they waited till it was night. The magician lay down in bed and put the bronze ring into his mouth, and very soon he was asleep.

"Now, what shall we do?" said the two little animals to each other.

The mouse with the cropped ears found a lamp full of oil, and a bottle full of pepper. So she dipped her tail first in the oil and then in the pepper, and held it to the man's nose.

"Atisha! atisha!" he sneezed, but he did not wake, and the shock made the bronze ring jump out of his mouth. Quick as thought the lame mouse snatched up the precious talisman and carried it off to the boat.

Imagine the despair of the magician when he awoke and the bronze ring was nowhere to be found!

But by that time our three mice had set sail with their prize. A favoring breeze was carrying them towards the island where the queen of the mice was awaiting them. Naturally they began to talk about the bronze ring.

"Which of us deserves the most credit?" they cried all at once.

"I do," said the blind mouse, "for without my watchfulness our boat would have drifted away to the open sea."

"No, indeed," cried the mouse with the cropped ears; "the credit is mine. Did I not cause the ring to jump out of the man's mouth?"

"No, it is mine," cried the lame one, "for I ran off with the ring."

And from high words they soon came to blows, and, alas! when the quarrel was fiercest the bronze ring fell into the sea.

"How are we to face our queen," said the three mice, "when by our folly we have lost the talisman and condemned our people to be utterly exterminated? We cannot go back to our country; let us land on this desert island and there end our miserable lives." No sooner said than done. The boat reached the island, and the mice landed.

The blind mouse was speedily deserted by her two sisters, who went off to hunt flies, but as she wandered sadly along the shore she found a dead fish, and was eating it, when she felt something very hard. At her cries the other two mice ran up.

"It is the bronze ring! It is the talisman!" they cried joyfully, and, getting into their boat again, they soon reached the mouse island. It was time they did, for the captain was just going to land his cargo of cats, when a deputation of mice brought him the precious bronze ring.

"Bronze ring," commanded the young man, "obey thy master. Let my ship appear as it was before."

Immediately the genii of the ring set to work, and the old black vessel became once more the wonderful golden ship with sails of brocade; the handsome sailors ran to the silver masts and the silken ropes, and very soon they set sail for the capital.

Ah! how merrily the sailors sang as they flew over the glassy sea!

At last the port was reached.

The captain landed and ran to the palace, where he found the magician asleep. The Princess clasped her husband in a long embrace. The magician tried to escape, but he was seized and bound with strong cords.

The next day the magician, tied to the tail of a savage mule loaded with nuts, was broken into as many pieces as there were nuts upon the mule's back.

Felicia and the Pot of Pinks

ONCE UPON A TIME there was a poor laborer who, feeling that he had not much longer to live, wished to divide his possessions between his son and daughter, whom he loved dearly.

So he called them to him, and said: "Your mother brought me as her dowry two stools and a straw bed; I have, besides, a hen, a pot of pinks, and a silver ring, which were given me by a noble lady who once lodged in my poor cottage. When she went away she said to me:

"'Be careful of my gifts, good man; see that you do not lose the ring or forget to water the pinks. As for your daughter, I promise you that she shall be more beautiful than anyone you ever saw in your life; call her Felicia, and when she grows up give her the ring and the pot of pinks to console her for her poverty.' Take them both then, my dear child," he added, "and your brother shall have everything else."

The two children seemed quite contented, and when their father died they wept for him, and divided his possessions as he had told them. Felicia believed that her brother loved her, but when she sat down upon one of the stools he said angrily:

"Keep your pot of pinks and your ring, but let my things alone. I like order in my house."

Felicia, who was very gentle, said nothing, but stood up crying quietly; while Bruno, for that was her brother's name, sat comfortably by the fire. Presently, when supper-time came, Bruno had a delicious egg, and he threw the shell to Felicia, saying:

"There, that is all I can give you; if you don't like it, go out and catch frogs; there are plenty of them in the marsh close by." Felicia did not answer, but she cried more bitterly than ever, and went away to her own little room. She found it filled with the sweet scent of the pinks, and, going up to them, she said sadly:

"Beautiful pinks, you are so sweet and so pretty, you are the only comfort I have left. Be very sure that I will

Felicia cried more bitterly than ever.

take care of you, and water you well, and never allow any cruel hand to tear you from your stems."

As she leant over them she noticed that they were very dry. So taking her pitcher, she ran off in the clear moonlight to the fountain, which was at some distance. When she reached it she sat down upon the brink to rest, but she had hardly done so when she saw a stately lady coming towards her, surrounded by numbers of attendants. Six maids of honor carried her train, and she leaned upon the arm of another.

When they came near the fountain a canopy was spread for her, under which was placed a sofa of cloth-of-gold, and presently a dainty supper was served, upon a table covered with dishes of gold and crystal, while the wind in the trees and the falling water of the fountains murmured the softest music.

Felicia was hidden in the shade, too much astonished by all she saw to venture to move; but in a few moments the Queen said:

"I fancy I see a shepherdess near that tree; bid her come hither."

So Felicia came forward and saluted the Queen timidly, but with so much grace that all were surprised.

"What are you doing here, my pretty child?" asked the Queen. "Are you not afraid of robbers?"

"Ah! madam," said Felicia, "a poor shepherdess who has nothing to lose does not fear robbers."

"You are not very rich, then?" said the Queen, smiling.

"I am so poor," answered Felicia, "that a pot of pinks and a silver ring are my only possessions in the world."

"But you have a heart," said the Queen. "What should you say if anybody wanted to steal that?"

"I do not know what it is like to lose one's heart, madam," she replied; "but I have always heard that without a heart one cannot live, and if it is broken one must die; and in spite of my poverty I should be sorry not to live."

"You are quite right to take care of your heart, pretty one," said the Queen. "But tell me, have you supped?"

"No, madam," answered Felicia; "my brother ate all the supper there was."

Then the Queen ordered that a place should be made for her at the table, and she herself loaded Felicia's plate with good things; but she was too much astonished to be hungry.

"I want to know what you were doing at the fountain so late?" said the Queen presently.

"I came to fetch a pitcher of water for my pinks, madam," she answered, stooping to pick up the pitcher which stood beside her; but when she showed it to the Queen she was amazed to see that it had turned to gold, all sparkling with great diamonds, and the water, of which it was full, was more fragrant than the sweetest roses. She was afraid to take it until the Queen said:

"It is yours, Felicia; go and water your pinks with it, and let it remind you that the Queen of the Woods is your friend."

The shepherdess threw herself at the Queen's feet, and thanked her humbly for her gracious words.

"Ah! madam," she cried, "if I might beg you to stay here a moment I would run and fetch my pot of pinks for you—they could not fall into better hands."

"Go, Felicia," said the Queen, stroking her cheek softly; "I will wait here until you come back."

So Felicia took up her pitcher and ran to her little room, but while she had been away Bruno had gone in and taken the pot of pinks, leaving a great cabbage in its place. When she saw the unlucky cabbage Felicia was much distressed, and did not know what to do; but

Felicia said: "I beg you to accept my ring."

at last she ran back to the fountain, and, kneeling before the Queen, said:

"Madam, Bruno has stolen my pot of pinks, so I have nothing but my silver ring; but I beg you to accept it as a proof of my gratitude."

"But if I take your ring, my pretty shepherdess," said the Queen, "you will have nothing left; and what will you do then?"

"Ah! madam," she answered simply, "if I have your friendship I shall do very well."

So the Queen took the ring and put it on her finger, and mounted her chariot, which was made of coral studded with emeralds, and drawn by six milk-white horses. And Felicia looked after her until the winding of the forest path hid her from her sight, and then she went back to the cottage, thinking over all the wonderful things that had happened.

The first thing she did when she reached her room was to throw the cabbage out of the window.

But she was very much surprised to hear an odd little voice cry out: "Oh! I am half killed!" and could not tell where it came from, because cabbages do not generally speak.

As soon as it was light, Felicia, who was very unhappy about her pot of pinks, went out to look for it, and the first thing she found was the unfortunate cabbage. She gave it a push with her foot, saying: "What are you doing here, and how dared you put yourself in the place of my pot of pinks?"

"If I hadn't been carried," replied the cabbage, "you may be very sure that I shouldn't have thought of going there."

It made her shiver with fright to hear the cabbage talk, but he went on:

"If you will be good enough to plant me by my comrades again, I can tell you where your pinks are at this moment—hidden in Bruno's bed!"

Felicia was in despair when she heard this, not knowing how she was to get them back. But she replanted the cabbage very kindly in his old place, and, as she finished doing it, she saw Bruno's hen, and said, catching hold of it:

"Come here, horrid little creature! you shall suffer for all the unkind things my brother has done to me."

"Ah! shepherdess," said the hen, "don't kill me; I am rather a gossip, and I can tell you some surprising things that you will like to hear. Don't imagine that you are the daughter of the poor laborer who brought you up; your mother was a queen who had six girls already, and the King threatened that unless she had a son who could inherit his kingdom she should have her head cut off.

"So when the Queen had another little daughter she was quite frightened, and agreed with her sister (who was a fairy) to exchange her for the fairy's little son. Now the Queen had been shut up in a great tower by the King's orders, and when a great many days went by and still she heard nothing from the Fairy she made her escape from the window by means of a rope ladder, taking her little baby with her. After wandering about until she was half dead with cold and fatigue she reached this cottage. I was the laborer's wife, and was a good nurse, and the Queen gave you into my charge, and told me all her misfortunes, and then died before she had time to say what was to become of you.

She made her escape, taking her baby with her.

"As I never in all my life could keep a secret, I could not help telling this strange tale to my neighbors, and one day a beautiful lady came here, and I told it to her also. When I had finished she touched me with a wand she held in her hand, and instantly I became a hen, and there was an end of my talking! I was very sad, and my husband, who was out when it happened, never knew what had become of me. After seeking me everywhere he believed that I must have been drowned, or eaten up by wild beasts in the forest. That same lady came here once more, and commanded that you should be called Felicia, and left the ring and the pot of pinks to be given to you; and while she was in the house twenty-five of the King's guards came to search for you, doubtless meaning to kill you; but she muttered a few words, and immediately they all turned into cabbages. It was one of them whom you threw out of your window yesterday.

"I don't know how it was that he could speak—I have never heard either of them say a word before, nor have I been able to do it myself until now."

The Princess was greatly astonished at the hen's story, and said kindly: "I am truly sorry for you, my poor nurse, and wish it was in my power to restore you to your real form. But we must not despair; it seems to me, after what you have told me, that something must be going to happen soon. Just now, however, I must go and look for my pinks, which I love better than anything in the world."

Bruno had gone out into the forest, never thinking that Felicia would search in his room for the pinks, and she was delighted by his unexpected absence, and thought to get them back without further trouble. But as soon as she entered the room she saw a terrible army of rats, who were guarding the straw bed; and when she attempted to approach it they sprang at her, biting and scratching furiously. Quite terrified, she drew back, crying out: "Oh! my dear pinks, how can you stay here in such bad company?"

Then she suddenly bethought herself of the pitcher of water, and, hoping that it might have some magic power, she ran to fetch it, and sprinkled a few drops over the fierce-looking swarm of rats. In a moment not a tail or a whisker was to be seen. Each one had made for his hole as fast as his legs could carry him, so that the Princess could safely take her pot of pinks. She found them nearly dying for want of water, and hastily poured all that was left in the pitcher upon them. As she bent over them, enjoying their delicious scent, a soft voice, that seemed to rustle among the leaves, said:

"Lovely Felicia, the day has come at last when I may have the happiness of telling you how even the flowers love you and rejoice in your beauty."

The Princess, quite overcome by the strangeness of hearing a cabbage, a hen, and a pink speak, and by the terrible sight of an army of rats, suddenly became very pale, and fainted away.

At this moment in came Bruno. Working hard in the heat had not improved his temper, and when he saw that Felicia had succeeded in finding her pinks he was so angry that he dragged her out into the garden and shut the door upon her. The fresh air soon made her open her pretty eyes, and there before her stood the Queen of the Woods, looking as charming as ever.

"You have a bad brother," she said; "I saw how cruelly he turned you out. Shall I punish him for it?"

"Ah! no, madam," she said; "I am not angry with him."

"But supposing he was not your brother, after all, what would you say then?" asked the Queen.

"Oh! but I think he must be," said Felicia.

"What!" said the Queen, "have you not heard that you are a princess?"

"I was told so a little while ago, madam, but how could I believe it without a single proof?"

"Ah! dear child," said the Queen, "the way you speak assures me that, in spite of your humble upbringing, you are indeed a real princess, and I can save you from being treated in such a way again."

She was interrupted at this moment by the arrival of a very handsome young man. He wore a coat of green velvet fastened with emerald clasps, and had a crown of pinks on his head. He knelt upon one knee and kissed the Queen's hand.

"Ah!" she cried, "my pink, my dear son, what a happiness to see you restored to your natural shape by Felicia's aid!" And she embraced him joyfully. Then turning to Felicia she said:

"Charming Princess, I know all the hen told you, but you cannot have heard that the zephyrs, to whom was entrusted the task of carrying my son to the tower where the Queen, your mother, so anxiously waited for him, left him instead in a garden of flowers, while they flew off to tell your mother. Whereupon a fairy with whom I had quarrelled changed him into a pink, and I could do nothing to prevent it.

"You may imagine how angry I was, and how I tried to find some means of undoing the mischief she had done; but there was no help for it. I could only bring Prince Pink to the place where you were being brought up, hoping that when you grew up he might love you, and by your care be restored to his natural form. And you see everything has come right, as I hoped it would. Your giving me the silver ring was the sign that the power of the charm was nearly over, and my enemy's last chance was to frighten you with her army of rats. That she did not succeed in doing; so now, my dear Felicia, if you will be married to my son with this silver ring your future happiness is certain. Do you think him handsome and amiable enough to be willing to marry him?"

"Madam," replied Felicia, blushing, "you overwhelm me with your kindness. I know that you are my mother's sister, and that by your art you turned the soldiers who were sent to kill me into cabbages, and my nurse into a hen, and that you do me only too much honor in proposing that I shall marry your son. How can I explain to you the cause of my hesitation? I feel, for the first time in my life, how happy it would make me to be beloved. Can you indeed give me the Prince's heart?"

"It is yours already, lovely Princess!" he cried, taking her hand .in his; "but for the horrible enchantment which kept me silent I should have told you long ago how dearly I love you."

This made the Princess very happy, and the Queen, who could not bear to see her dressed like a poor shepherdess, touched her with her wand, saying:

"I wish you to be attired as befits your rank and beauty." And immediately the Princess's cotton dress became a magnificent robe of silver brocade embroidered with carbuncles, and her soft dark hair was encircled by a crown of diamonds, from which floated a clear white veil. With her bright eyes, and the charming color in her cheeks, she was altogether such a dazzling sight that the Prince could hardly bear it.

"How pretty you are, Felicia!" he cried. "Don't keep me in suspense, I entreat you; say that you will marry me."

"Ah!" said the Queen, smiling, "I think she will not refuse now."

Just then Bruno, who was going back to his work, came out of the cottage, and thought he must be dreaming when he saw Felicia; but she called him very kindly, and begged the Queen to take pity on him.

"What!" she said, "when he was so unkind to you?"

"Ah! madam," said the Princess, "I am so happy that I should like everybody else to be happy too."

The Queen kissed her, and said: "Well, to please you, let me see what I can do for this cross Bruno." And with a wave of her wand she turned the poor little cottage into a splendid palace, full of treasures; only the two stools and the straw bed remained just as they were, to remind him of his former poverty. Then the Queen touched Bruno himself, and made him gentle and polite and grateful, and he thanked her and the Princess a thousand times. Lastly, the Queen restored the hen and the cabbages to their natural forms, and left them all very contented. The Prince and Princess were married as soon as possible with great splendor, and lived happily ever after.

The White Cat

ONCE UPON A TIME there was a king who had three sons, who were all so clever and brave that he began to be afraid that they would want to reign over the kingdom before he was dead. Now the King, though he felt that he was growing old, did not at all wish to give up the government of his kingdom while he could still manage it very well, so he thought the best way to live in peace would be to divert the minds of his sons by promises which he could always get out of when the time came for keeping them.

So he sent for them all, and, after speaking to them kindly, he added:

"You will quite agree with me, my dear children, that my great age makes it impossible for me to look after my affairs of state as carefully as I once did. I begin to fear that this may affect the welfare of my subjects, therefore I wish that one of you should succeed to my crown; but in return for such a gift as this it is only right that you should do something for me. Now, as I think of retiring into the country, it seems to me that a pretty, lively, faithful little dog would be very good company for me; so, without any regard for your ages, I promise that the one who brings me the most beautiful little dog shall succeed me at once."

The three Princes were greatly surprised by their father's sudden fancy for a little dog, but as it gave the two younger ones a chance they would not otherwise have had of being king, and as the eldest was too polite to make any objection, they accepted the commission with pleasure. They bade farewell to the King, who gave them presents of silver and precious stones, and appointed to meet them at the same hour, in the same place, after a year had passed, to see the little dogs they had brought for him.

Then they went together to a castle which was about a league from the city, accompanied by all their particular friends, to whom they gave a grand banquet, and the three brothers promised to be friends always, to share whatever good fortune befell them, and not to be parted by any envy or jealousy; and so they set out, agreeing to meet at the same castle at the appointed time, to present themselves before the King together. Each one took a different road, and the two eldest met with many adventures; but it is about the youngest that you are going to hear. He was young, and gay, and handsome, and knew everything that a prince ought to know; and as for his courage, there was simply no end to it.

Hardly a day passed without his buying several dogs—big and little, greyhounds, mastiffs, spaniels, and lapdogs. As soon as he had bought a pretty one he was sure to see a still prettier, and then he had to get rid of all the others and buy that one, as, being alone, he found it impossible to take thirty or forty thousand dogs about with him. He journeyed from day to day, not knowing where he was going, until at last, just at nightfall, he reached a great, gloomy forest. He did not know

At length he reached the door of a splendid castle.

his way, and, to make matters worse, it began to thunder, and the rain poured down. He took the first path he could find, and after walking for a long time he fancied he saw a faint light, and began to hope that he was coming to some cottage where he might find shelter for the night. At length, guided by the light, he reached the door of the most splendid castle he could have imagined. This door was of gold covered with carbuncles, and it was the pure red light which shone from them that had shown him the way through the forest. The walls were of the finest porcelain in all the most delicate colors, and the Prince saw that all the stories he had ever read were pictured upon them; but as he was quite terribly wet, and the rain still fell in torrents, he could not stay to look about any more, but came back to the golden door. There he saw a deer's foot hanging by a chain of diamonds, and he began to wonder who could live in this magnificent castle.

"They must feel very secure against robbers," he said to himself. "What is to hinder anyone from cutting off that chain and digging out those carbuncles, and making himself rich for life?"

He pulled the deer's foot, and immediately a silver bell sounded and the door flew open, but the Prince could see nothing but numbers of hands in the air, each holding a torch. He was so much surprised that he stood quite still, until he felt himself pushed forward by other hands, so that, though he was somewhat uneasy, he could not help going on. With his hand on his sword, to be prepared for whatever might happen, he entered a hall paved with lapis-lazuli, while two lovely voices sang:

> The hands you see floating above
>   Will swiftly your bidding obey;
> If your heart dreads not conquering Love,
>   In this place you may fearlessly stay.

The Prince could not believe that any danger threatened him when he was welcomed in this way, so, guided by the mysterious hands, he went towards a door of coral, which opened of its own accord, and he found himself in a vast hall of mother-of-pearl, out of which opened a number of other rooms, glittering with thousands of lights, and full of such beautiful pictures and precious things that the Prince felt quite bewildered. After passing through sixty rooms the hands that conducted him stopped, and the Prince saw a most comfortable-looking arm-chair drawn up close to the chimney-corner; at the same moment the fire lighted itself, and the pretty, soft, clever hands took off the Prince's wet, muddy clothes, and presented him with fresh ones made of the richest stuffs, all embroidered with gold and emeralds. He could not help admiring everything he saw, and the deft way in which the hands waited on him, though they sometimes appeared so suddenly that they made him jump.

When he was quite ready—and I can assure you that he looked very different from the wet and weary Prince who had stood outside in the rain, and pulled the deer's foot—the hands led him to a splendid room, upon the walls of which were painted the histories of Puss in Boots and a number of other famous cats. The table was laid for supper with two golden plates, and golden spoons and forks, and the sideboard was covered with dishes and glasses of crystal set with precious stones. The Prince was wondering who the second place could be for, when suddenly in came about a dozen cats carrying guitars and rolls of music, who took their places at one end of the room, and under the direction of a cat who beat time with a roll of paper began to mew in every imaginable key, and to draw their claws across the strings of the guitars, making the strangest kind of music that could be heard. The Prince hastily stopped up his ears, but even then the sight of these comical musicians sent him into fits of laughter.

"What funny thing shall I see next?" he said to himself, and instantly the door opened, and in came a tiny figure covered by a long black veil. It was conducted by two cats wearing black mantles and carrying swords, and a large party of cats followed, who brought in cages full of rats and mice.

The Prince was so much astonished that he thought he must be dreaming, but the little figure came up to him and threw back its veil, and he saw that it was the loveliest little white cat it is possible to imagine. She looked very young and very sad, and in a sweet little voice that went straight to his heart she said to the Prince:

"King's son, you are welcome; the Queen of the Cats is glad to see you."

"Lady Cat," replied the Prince, "I thank you for receiving me so kindly, but surely you are no ordinary pussy-cat? Indeed, the way you speak and the magnificence of your castle prove it plainly."

"King's son," said the White Cat, "I beg you to spare me these compliments, for I am not used to them. But now," she added, "let supper be served, and let the musicians be silent, as the Prince does not understand what they are saying."

It was the loveliest cat it is possible to imagine.

So the mysterious hands began to bring in the supper, and first they put on the table two dishes, one containing stewed pigeons and the other a fricassée of fat mice. The sight of the latter made the Prince feel as if he could not enjoy his supper at all; but the White Cat seeing this assured him that the dishes intended for him were prepared in a separate kitchen, and he might be quite certain that they contained neither rats nor mice; and the Prince felt so sure that she would not deceive him that he had no more hesitation in beginning. Presently he noticed that on the little paw that was next him the White Cat wore a bracelet containing a portrait, and he begged to be allowed to look at it. To his great surprise he found it represented an extremely handsome young man, who was so like himself that it might have been his own portrait! The White Cat sighed as he looked at it, and seemed sadder than ever, and the Prince dared not ask any questions for fear of displeasing her; so he began to talk about other things, and found that she was interested in all the subjects he cared for himself, and seemed to know quite well what was going on in the world. After supper they went into another room, which was fitted up as a theatre, and the cats acted and danced for their amusement, and then the White Cat said good-night to him, and the hands conducted him into a room he had not seen before, hung with tapestry worked with butterflies' wings of every color; there were mirrors that reached from the ceiling to the floor, and a little white bed with curtains of gauze tied up with ribbons. The Prince went to bed in silence, as he did not quite know how to begin a conversation with the hands that waited on him, and in the morning he was awakened by a noise and confusion outside his window, and the hands came and quickly dressed him in hunting costume. When he looked out

The White Cat herself was riding a monkey.

all the cats were assembled in the courtyard, some leading greyhounds, some blowing horns, for the White Cat was going out hunting. The hands led a wooden horse up to the Prince, and seemed to expect him to mount it, at which he was very indignant; but it was no use for him to object, for he speedily found himself upon its back, and it pranced gaily off with him.

The White Cat herself was riding a monkey, which climbed even up to the eagles' nests when she had a fancy for the young eaglets. Never was there a pleasanter hunting party, and when they returned to the castle the Prince and the White Cat supped together as before, but when they had finished she offered him a crystal goblet, which must have contained a magic draught, for, as soon as he had swallowed its contents, he forgot everything, even the little dog that he was seeking for the King, and only thought how happy he was to be with the White Cat! And so the days passed, in every kind of amusement, until the year was nearly gone. The Prince had forgotten all about meeting his brothers: he did not even know what country he belonged to; but the White Cat knew when he ought to go back, and one day she said to him:

"Do you know that you have only three days left to look for the little dog for your father, and your brothers have found lovely ones?"

Then the Prince suddenly recovered his memory, and cried:

"What can have made me forget such an important thing? my whole fortune depends upon it; and even if I could in such a short time find a dog pretty enough to gain me a kingdom, where should I find a horse who could carry me all that way in three days?" And he began to be very vexed. But the White Cat said to him: "King's son, do not trouble yourself; I am your friend, and will make everything easy for you. You can still stay here for a day, as the good wooden horse can take you to your country in twelve hours."

"I thank you, beautiful Cat," said the Prince; "but what good will it do me to get back if I have not a dog to take to my father?"

"See here," answered the White Cat, holding up an acorn; "there is a prettier one in this than in the Dog-star!"

"Oh! White Cat dear," said the Prince, "how unkind you are to laugh at me now!"

"Only listen," she said, holding the acorn to his ear.

And inside it he distinctly heard a tiny voice say: "Bow-wow!"

The Prince was delighted, for a dog that can be shut up in an acorn must be very small indeed. He wanted to take it out and look at it, but the White Cat said it would be better not to open the acorn till he was before the King, in case the tiny dog should be cold on the journey. He thanked her a thousand times, and said goodbye quite sadly when the time came for him to set out.

"The days have passed so quickly with you," he said, "I only wish I could take you with me now."

But the White Cat shook her head and sighed deeply in answer.

After all the Prince was the first to arrive at the castle where he had agreed to meet his brothers, but they came soon after, and stared in amazement when they saw the wooden horse in the courtyard jumping like a hunter.

The Prince met them joyfully, and they began to tell him all their adventures; but he managed to hide from them what he had been doing, and even led them to think that a turnspit dog which he had with him was the one he was bringing for the King. Fond as they all were of one another, the two eldest could not help being glad to think that their dogs certainly had a better chance. The next morning they started in the same chariot. The elder brothers carried in baskets two such tiny, fragile dogs that they hardly dared to touch them. As for the turnspit, he ran after the chariot, and got so covered with mud that one could hardly see what he was like at all. When they reached the palace everyone crowded round to welcome them as they went into the King's great hall; and when the two brothers presented their little dogs nobody could decide which was the prettier. They were already arranging between themselves to share the kingdom equally, when the youngest stepped forward, drawing from his pocket the acorn the White Cat had given him. He opened it quickly, and there upon a white cushion they saw a dog so small that it could easily have been put through a ring. The Prince laid it upon the ground, and it got up at once and began to dance. The King did not know what to say, for it was impossible that anything could be prettier than this little creature. Nevertheless, as he was in no hurry to part with his crown, he told his sons that, as they had been so successful the first time, he would ask them to go once again, and seek by land and sea for a piece of muslin so fine that it could be drawn through the eye of a needle. The brothers were not very willing to set out again, but the two eldest consented because it gave them another chance, and they started as

The little dog got up and began to dance.

before. The youngest again mounted the wooden horse, and rode back at full speed to his beloved White Cat. Every door of the castle stood wide open, and every window and turret was illuminated, so it looked more wonderful than before. The hands hastened to meet him, and led the wooden horse off to the stable, while he hurried in to find the White Cat. She was asleep in a little basket on a white satin cushion, but she very soon started up when she heard the Prince, and was over-joyed at seeing him once more.

"How could I hope that you would come back to me, King's son?" she said. And then he stroked and petted her, and told her of his successful journey, and how he had come back to ask her help, as he believed that it was impossible to find what the King demanded. The White Cat looked serious, and said she must think what was to be done, but that, luckily, there were some cats in the castle who could spin very well, and if anybody could manage it they could, and she would set them the task herself.

And then the hands appeared carrying torches, and conducted the Prince and the White Cat to a long gallery which overlooked the river, from the windows of which they saw a magnificent display of fireworks of all sorts; after which they had supper, which the Prince liked even better than the fireworks, for it was very late, and he was hungry after his long ride. And so the days passed quickly as before; it was impossible to feel dull with the White Cat, and she had quite a talent for inventing new amusements—indeed, she was cleverer than a cat has any right to be. But when the Prince asked her how it was that she was so wise, she only said:

"King's son, do not ask me; guess what you please. I may not tell you anything."

The Prince was so happy that he did not trouble himself at all about the time, but presently the White Cat told him that the year was gone, and that he need not be at all anxious about the piece of muslin, as they had made it very well.

"This time," she added, "I can give you a suitable escort;" and on looking out into the courtyard the Prince saw a superb chariot of burnished gold, enamelled in flame color with a thousand different designs. It was drawn by twelve snow-white horses, harnessed four abreast; their trappings were of flame-colored velvet, embroidered with diamonds. A hundred chariots followed, each drawn by eight horses, and filled with officers in splendid uniforms, and a thousand guards surrounded the procession. "Go!" said the White Cat, "and when you appear before the King in such state he surely will not refuse you the crown which you deserve. Take this walnut, but do not open it until you are before him, then you will find in it the piece of stuff you asked me for."

"Lovely Blanchette," said the Prince, "how can I thank you properly for all your kindness to me? Only tell me that you wish it, and I will give up for ever all thought of being king, and will stay here with you always."

"King's son," she replied, "it shows the goodness of your heart that you should care so much for a little white cat, who is good for nothing but to catch mice; but you must not stay."

So the Prince kissed her little paw and set out. You can imagine how fast he travelled when I tell you that they reached the King's palace in just half the time it had taken the wooden horse to get there. This time the Prince was so late that he did not try to meet his brothers at their castle, so they thought he could not be coming, and were rather glad of it, and displayed their pieces of muslin to the King proudly, feeling sure of success. And indeed the stuff was very fine, and would go through the eye of a very large needle; but the King, who was only too glad to make a difficulty, sent for a particular needle, which was kept among the Crown jewels, and had such a small eye that everybody saw at once that it was impossible that the muslin should pass through it. The Princes were angry, and were beginning to complain that it was a trick, when suddenly the trumpets sounded and the youngest Prince came in. His father and brothers were quite astonished at his magnificence, and after he had greeted them he took the walnut from his pocket and opened it, fully expecting to find the piece of muslin, but instead there was only a hazel-nut. He cracked it, and there lay a cherrystone. Everybody was looking on, and the King was chuckling to himself at the idea of finding the piece of muslin in a nutshell.

However, the Prince cracked the cherry-stone, but everyone laughed when he saw it contained only its own kernel. He opened that and found a grain of wheat, and in that was a millet seed. Then he himself began to wonder, and muttered softly:

"White Cat, White Cat, are you making fun of me?"

In an instant he felt a cat's claw give his hand quite a sharp scratch, and hoping that it was meant as an encouragement he opened the millet seed, and drew out of it a piece of muslin four hundred ells long, woven with the loveliest colors and most wonderful patterns; and when the needle was brought it went through the eye six times with the greatest ease! The King turned pale, and the other Princes stood silent and sorrowful, for nobody could deny that this was the most marvellous piece of muslin that was to be found in the world.

Presently the King turned to his sons, and said, with a deep sigh:

"Nothing could console me more in my old age than to realise your willingness to gratify my wishes. Go then once more, and whoever at the end of a year can bring back the loveliest princess shall be married to her, and shall, without further delay, receive the crown, for my successor must certainly be married." The Prince considered that he had earned the kingdom fairly twice over, but still he was too well bred to argue about it, so he just went back to his gorgeous chariot, and, surrounded by his escort, returned to the White Cat faster than he had come. This time she was expecting him, the path was strewn with flowers, and a thousand braziers were burning scented woods which perfumed the air. Seated in a gallery from which she could see his arrival, the White Cat waited for him. "Well, King's son," she said, "here you are once more, without a crown." "Madam," said he, "thanks to your generosity I have earned one twice over; but the fact is that my father is so loth to part with it that it would be no pleasure to me to take it."

"Never mind," she answered; "it's just as well to try and deserve it. As you must take back a lovely princess with you next time I will be on the look-out for one for you. In the meantime let us enjoy ourselves; to-night I have ordered a battle between my cats and the river rats, on purpose to amuse you." So this year slipped away even more pleasantly than the preceding ones. Sometimes the Prince could not help asking the White Cat how it was she could talk.

"Perhaps you are a fairy," he said. "Or has some enchanter changed you into a cat?"

But she only gave him answers that told him nothing. Days go by so quickly when one is very happy that it is certain the Prince would never have thought of its being time to go back, when one evening as they sat together the White Cat said to him that if he wanted to take a lovely princess home with him the next day he must be prepared to do as she told him.

"Take this sword," she said, "and cut off my head!"

"I!" cried the Prince, "I cut off your head! Blanchette darling, how could I do it?"

"I entreat you to do as I tell you, King's son," she replied.

The tears came into the Prince's eyes as he begged her to ask him anything but that—to set him any task she pleased as a proof of his devotion, but to spare him

Suddenly a lovely princess stood before him.

the grief of killing his dear Pussy. But nothing he could say altered her determination, and at last he drew his sword, and desperately, with a trembling hand, cut off the little white head. But imagine his astonishment and delight when suddenly a lovely princess stood before him, and, while he was still speechless with amazement, the door opened and a goodly company of knights and ladies entered, each carrying a cat's skin! They hastened with every sign of joy to the Princess, kissing her hand and congratulating her on being once more restored to her natural shape. She received them graciously, but after a few minutes begged that they would leave her alone with the Prince, to whom she said:

"You see, Prince, that you were right in supposing me to be no ordinary cat. My father reigned over six kingdoms. The Queen, my mother, whom he loved dearly, had a passion for travelling and exploring, and when I was only a few weeks old she obtained his permission to visit a certain mountain of which she had heard many marvellous tales, and set out, taking with her a number of her attendants. On the way they had to pass near an old castle belonging to the fairies. Nobody had ever been into it, but it was reported to be full of the most wonderful things, and my mother remembered to have heard that the fairies had in their garden such fruits as were to be seen and tasted nowhere else. She began to wish to try them for herself, and turned her steps in the direction of the garden. On arriving at the door, which blazed with gold and jewels, she ordered her servants to knock loudly, but it was useless; it seemed as if all the inhabitants of the castle must be asleep or dead. Now the more difficult it became to obtain the fruit, the more the Queen was determined that have it she would. So she ordered that they should

A tiny woman was seated by her bedside.

bring ladders, and get over the wall into the garden; but though the wall did not look very high, and they tied the ladders together to make them very long, it was quite impossible to get to the top.

"The Queen was in despair, but as night was coming on she ordered that they should encamp just where they were, and went to bed herself, feeling quite ill, she was so disappointed. In the middle of the night she was suddenly awakened, and saw to her surprise a tiny, ugly old woman seated by her bedside, who said to her:

"'I must say that we consider it somewhat troublesome of your Majesty to insist upon tasting our fruit;

but, to save you any annoyance, my sisters and I will consent to give you as much as you can carry away, on one condition—that is, that you shall give us your little daughter to bring up as our own.'

"'Ah! my dear madam,' cried the Queen, 'is there nothing else that you will take for the fruit? I will give you my kingdoms willingly.'

"'No,' replied the old fairy, 'we will have nothing but your little daughter. She shall be as happy as the day is long, and we will give her everything that is worth having in fairy-land, but you must not see her again until she is married.'

"'Though it is a hard condition,' said the Queen, 'I consent, for I shall certainly die if I do not taste the fruit, and so I should lose my little daughter either way.'

The dragon ate up all the people he met.

"So the old fairy led her into the castle, and, though it was still the middle of the night, the Queen could see plainly that it was far more beautiful than she had been told, which you can easily believe, Prince," said the White Cat, "when I tell you that it was this castle that we are now in. 'Will you gather the fruit yourself, Queen?' said the old fairy, 'or shall I call it to come to you?'

"'I beg you to let me see it come when it is called,' cried the Queen; 'that will be something quite new.' The old fairy whistled twice, then she cried:

"'Apricots, peaches, nectarines, cherries, plums, pears, melons, grapes, apples, oranges, lemons, gooseberries, strawberries, raspberries, come!'

"And in an instant they came tumbling in, one over another, and yet they were neither dusty nor spoilt, and the Queen found them quite as good as she had fancied them. You see they grew upon fairy trees.

"The old fairy gave her golden baskets in which to take the fruit away, and it was as much as four hundred mules could carry. Then she reminded the Queen of her agreement, and led her back to the camp, and next morning she went back to her kingdom; but before she had gone very far she began to repent of her bargain, and when the King came out to meet her she looked so sad that he guessed that something had happened, and asked what was the matter. At first the Queen was afraid to tell him, but when, as soon as they reached the palace, five frightful little dwarfs were sent by the fairies to fetch me, she was obliged to confess what she had promised. The King was very angry, and had the Queen and myself shut up in a great tower and safely guarded, and drove the little dwarfs out of his kingdom; but the fairies sent a great dragon who ate up all the people he met, and whose breath burnt up everything as he passed through the country; and at last, after trying in vain to rid himself of the monster, the King, to save his subjects, was obliged to consent that I should be given up to the fairies. This time they came themselves to fetch me, in a chariot of pearl drawn by seahorses, followed by the dragon, who was led with chains of diamonds. My cradle was placed between the old fairies, who loaded me with caresses, and away we whirled through the air to a tower which they built on purpose for me. There I grew up surrounded with everything that was beautiful and rare, and learning everything that is ever taught to a princess, but without any companions but a parrot and a little dog, who could both talk; and receiving every day a visit from one of the old fairies, who came mounted upon the dragon. One day, however, as I sat at my window I saw a handsome young prince, who seemed to have been hunting in the forest which surrounded my prison, and who was standing and looking up at me. When he saw that I observed him he saluted me with great deference. You can imagine that I was delighted to have some one new to talk to, and in spite of the height of my window our conversation was prolonged till night fell, then my prince reluctantly bade me farewell. But after that he came again many times, and at last I consented to marry him, but the question was how I was to escape from my tower. The fairies always supplied me with flax for my spinning, and by great diligence I made enough cord for a ladder that would reach to the foot of the tower; but, alas! just as my prince was helping me to descend it, the crossest and ugliest of the old fairies flew in. Before he had time to defend himself my unhappy lover was swallowed up by the dragon. As for me, the fairies, furious at having their plans defeated, for they intended me to marry the king of the dwarfs and I

Just then the crossest of the fairies flew in.

utterly refused, changed me into a white cat. When they brought me here I found all the lords and ladies of my father's court awaiting me under the same enchantment, while the people of lesser rank had been made invisible, all but their hands.

"As they laid me under the enchantment the fairies told me all my history, for until then I had quite believed that I was their child, and warned me that my only chance of regaining my natural form was to win the love of a prince who resembled in every way my unfortunate lover."

"And you have won it, lovely Princess," interrupted the Prince.

"You are indeed wonderfully like him," resumed the Princess—"in voice, in features, and everything; and if you really love me all my troubles will be at an end."

They mounted the chariot together.

"And mine too," cried the Prince, throwing himself at her feet, "if you will consent to marry me."

"I love you already better than anyone in the world," she said; "but now it is time to go back to your father, and we shall hear what he says about it."

So the Prince gave her his hand and led her out, and they mounted the chariot together; it was even more splendid than before, and so was the whole company. Even the horses' shoes were of rubies with diamond nails, and I suppose that is the first time such a thing was ever seen.

As the Princess was as kind and clever as she was beautiful, you may imagine what a delightful journey the Prince found it, for everything the Princess said seemed to him quite charming.

When they came near the castle where the brothers were to meet, the Princess got into a chair carried by four of the guards; it was hewn out of one splendid crystal, and had silken curtains, which she drew round her that she might not be seen.

The Prince saw his brothers walking upon the terrace, each with a lovely princess, and they came to meet him, asking if he had also found a wife. He said that he had found something much rarer—a little white cat! At which they laughed very much, and asked him if he was afraid of being eaten up by mice in the palace. And then they set out together for the town. Each prince and princess rode in a splendid carriage; the horses were decked with plumes of feathers, and glittered with gold. After them came the youngest prince, and last of all the crystal chair, at which everybody looked with admiration and curiosity. When the courtiers saw them coming they hastened to tell the King.

"Are the ladies beautiful?" he asked anxiously.

And when they answered that nobody had ever before seen such lovely princesses he seemed quite annoyed.

However, he received them graciously, but found it impossible to choose between them.

Then turning to his youngest son he said:

"Have you come back alone, after all?"

"Your Majesty," replied the Prince, "will find in that crystal chair a little white cat, which has such soft paws, and mews so prettily, that I am sure you will be charmed with it."

The King smiled, and went to draw back the curtains himself, but at a touch from the Princess the crystal shivered into a thousand splinters, and there she stood in all her beauty; her fair hair floated over her shoulders and was crowned with flowers, and her softly falling robe was of the purest white. She saluted the King gracefully, while a murmur of admiration rose from all around.

"Sire," she said, "I am not come to deprive you of the throne you fill so worthily. I have already six kingdoms, permit me to bestow one upon you, and upon each of your sons. I ask nothing but your friendship, and your consent to my marriage with your youngest son; we shall still have three kingdoms left for ourselves."

The King and all the courtiers could not conceal their joy and astonishment, and the marriage of the three Princes was celebrated at once. The festivities lasted several months, and then each king and queen departed to their own kingdom and lived happily ever after.

The Story of Pretty Goldilocks

ONCE UPON A TIME there was a princess who was the prettiest creature in the world. And because she was so beautiful, and because her hair was like the finest gold, and waved and rippled nearly to the ground, she was called Pretty Goldilocks. She always wore a crown of flowers, and her dresses were embroidered with diamonds and pearls, and everybody who saw her fell in love with her.

Now one of her neighbors was a young king who was not married. He was very rich and handsome, and when he heard all that was said about Pretty Goldilocks, though he had never seen her, he fell so deeply in love with her that he could neither eat nor drink. So he resolved to send an ambassador to ask her in marriage. He had a splendid carriage made for his ambassador, and gave him more than a hundred horses and a hundred servants, and told him to be sure to bring the Princess back with him. After he had started nothing else was talked of at Court, and the King felt so sure that the Princess would consent that he set his people to work at pretty dresses and splendid furniture, that they might be ready by the time she came.

Meanwhile, the ambassador arrived at the Princess's palace and delivered his little message, but whether she happened to be cross that day, or whether the compliment did not please her, is not known. She only answered that she was very much obliged to the King, but she had no wish to be married. The ambassador set off sadly on his homeward way, bringing all the King's presents back with him, for the Princess was too well brought up to accept the pearls and diamonds when she would not accept the King, so she had only kept twenty-five English pins that he might not be vexed.

When the ambassador reached the city, where the King was waiting impatiently, everybody was very much annoyed with him for not bringing the Princess, and the King cried like a baby, and nobody could console him. Now there was at the Court a young man, who

The King cried like a baby.

was more clever and handsome than anyone else. He was called Charming, and everyone loved him, excepting a few envious people who were angry at his being the King's favorite and knowing all the State secrets. He happened one day to be with some people who were speaking of the ambassador's return and saying that his going to the Princess had not done much good, when Charming said rashly:

"If the King had sent me to the Princess Goldilocks I am sure she would have come back with me."

His enemies at once went to the King and said:

"You will hardly believe, sire, what Charming has the audacity to say—that if *he* had been sent to the Princess Goldilocks she would certainly have come back with him. He seems to think that he is so much handsomer than you that the Princess would have fallen in love with him and followed him willingly." The King was very angry when he heard this.

"Ha, ha!" said he; "does he laugh at my unhappiness, and think himself more fascinating than I am? Go, and let him be shut up in my great tower to die of hunger."

So the King's guards went to fetch Charming, who had thought no more of his rash speech, and carried him off to prison with great cruelty. The poor prisoner had only a little straw for his bed, and but for a little stream of water which flowed through the tower he would have died of thirst.

One day when he was in despair he said to himself:

"How can I have offended the King? I am his most faithful subject, and have done nothing against him."

The King chanced to be passing the tower and recognised the voice of his former favorite. He stopped to listen in spite of Charming's enemies, who tried to persuade him to have nothing more to do with the traitor. But the King said:

"Be quiet, I wish to hear what he says."

And then he opened the tower door and called to Charming, who came very sadly and kissed the King's hand, saying:

"What have I done, sire, to deserve this cruel treatment?"

"You mocked me and my ambassador," said the King, "and you said that if I had sent you for the Princess Goldilocks you would certainly have brought her back."

"It is quite true, sire," replied Charming; "I should have drawn such a picture of you, and represented your good qualities in such a way, that I am certain the Princess would have found you irresistible. But I cannot see what there is in that to make you angry."

The King could not see any cause for anger either when the matter was presented to him in this light, and he began to frown very fiercely at the courtiers who had so misrepresented his favorite.

So he took Charming back to the palace with him, and after seeing that he had a very good supper he said to him:

"You know that I love Pretty Goldilocks as much as ever, her refusal has not made any difference to me; but I don't know how to make her change her mind: I really should like to send you, to see if you can persuade her to marry me."

Charming replied that he was perfectly willing to go, and would set out the very next day.

"But you must wait till I can get a grand escort for you," said the King. But Charming said that he only wanted a good horse to ride, and the King, who was delighted at his being ready to start so promptly, gave him letters to the Princess, and bade him good speed. It was on a Monday morning that he set out all alone

He saw a golden carp lying upon the grass.

upon his errand, thinking of nothing but how he could persuade the Princess Goldilocks to marry the King. He had a writing-book in his pocket, and whenever any happy thought struck him he dismounted from his horse and sat down under the trees to put it into the harangue which he was preparing for the Princess, before he forgot it.

One day when he had started at the very earliest dawn, and was riding over a great meadow, he suddenly had a capital idea, and, springing from his horse, he sat down under a willow tree which grew by a little river. When he had written it down he was looking round him, pleased to find himself in such a pretty place, when all at once he saw a great golden carp lying gasping and exhausted upon the grass. In leaping after little flies she had thrown herself high upon the bank, where she had lain till she was nearly dead. Charming had pity upon her, and, though he couldn't help thinking that she would have been very nice for dinner, he picked her up gently and put her back into the water. As soon as Dame Carp felt the refreshing coolness of the water she sank down joyfully to the bottom of the river, then, swimming up to the bank quite boldly, she said:

"I thank you, Charming, for the kindness you have done me. You have saved my life; one day I will repay you." So saying, she sank down into the water again, leaving Charming greatly astonished at her politeness.

Another day, as he journeyed on, he saw a raven in great distress. The poor bird was closely pursued by an eagle, which would soon have eaten it up, had not Charming quickly fitted an arrow to his bow and shot the eagle dead. The raven perched upon a tree very joyfully.

"Charming," said he, "it was very generous of you to rescue a poor raven; I am not ungrateful, some day I will repay you."

Charming thought it was very nice of the raven to say so, and went on his way.

Before the sun rose he found himself in a thick wood where it was too dark for him to see his path, and here he heard an owl crying as if it were in despair.

"Hark!" said he, "that must be an owl in great trouble, I am sure it has got into a snare;" and he began to hunt about, and presently found a great net which some bird-catchers had spread the night before.

"What a pity it is that men do nothing but torment and persecute poor creatures which never do them any harm!" said he, and he took out his knife and cut the cords of the net, and the owl flitted away into the darkness, but then turning, with one flicker of her wings, she came back to Charming and said:

"It does not need many words to tell you how great a service you have done me. I was caught; in a few minutes the fowlers would have been here—without your help I should have been killed. I am grateful, and one day I will repay you."

These three adventures were the only ones of any consequence that befell Charming upon his journey, and he made all the haste he could to reach the palace of the Princess Goldilocks.

When he arrived he thought everything he saw delightful and magnificent. Diamonds were as plentiful as pebbles, and the gold and silver, the beautiful dresses, the sweetmeats and pretty things that were everywhere quite amazed him; he thought to himself: "If the Princess consents to leave all this, and come with me to marry the King, he may think himself lucky!"

Then he dressed himself carefully in rich brocade, with scarlet and white plumes, and threw a splendid embroidered scarf over his shoulder, and, looking as gay and as graceful as possible, he presented himself at the door of the palace, carrying in his arm a tiny pretty dog which he had bought on the way. The guards saluted him respectfully, and a messenger was sent to the Princess to announce the arrival of Charming as ambassador of her neighbor the King.

"Charming," said the Princess, "the name promises well; I have no doubt that he is good-looking and fascinates everybody."

"Indeed he does, madam," said all her maids of honor in one breath. "We saw him from the window of the garret where we were spinning flax, and we could do nothing but look at him as long as he was in sight."

"Well to be sure!" said the Princess, "that's how you amuse yourselves, is it? Looking at strangers out of the window! Be quick and give me my blue satin embroi-

dered dress, and comb out my golden hair. Let somebody make me fresh garlands of flowers, and give me
my high-heeled shoes and my fan, and tell them to
sweep my great hall and my throne, for I want everyone
to say I am really 'Pretty Goldilocks.'"

You can imagine how all her maids scurried this way
and that to make the Princess ready, and how in their
haste they knocked their heads together and hindered
each other, till she thought they would never have
done. However, at last they led her into the gallery of
mirrors that she might assure herself that nothing was
lacking in her appearance, and then she mounted her
throne of gold, ebony, and ivory, while her ladies took
their guitars and began to sing softly. Then Charming
was led in, and was so struck with astonishment and

He took courage and delivered his harangue.

admiration that at first not a word could he say. But presently he took courage and delivered his harangue, bravely ending by begging the Princess to spare him the disappointment of going back without her.

"Sir Charming," answered she, "all the reasons you have given me are very good ones, and I assure you that I should have more pleasure in obliging you than anyone else, but you must know that a month ago as I was walking by the river with my ladies I took off my glove, and as I did so a ring that I was wearing slipped off my finger and rolled into the water. As I valued it more than my kingdom, you may imagine how vexed I was at losing it, and I vowed never to listen to any proposal of marriage unless the ambassador first brought me back my ring. So now you know what is expected of you, for if you talked for fifteen days and fifteen nights you could not make me change my mind."

Charming was very much surprised by this answer, but he bowed low to the Princess, and begged her to accept the embroidered scarf and the tiny dog he had brought with him. But she answered that she did not want any presents, and that he was to remember what she had just told him. When he got back to his lodging he went to bed without eating any supper, and his little dog, who was called Frisk, couldn't eat any either, but came and lay down close to him. All night long Charming sighed and lamented.

"How am I to find a ring that fell into the river a month ago?" said he. "It is useless to try; the Princess must have told me to do it on purpose, knowing it was impossible." And then he sighed again.

Frisk heard him and said:

"My dear master, don't despair; the luck may change, you are too good not to be happy. Let us go down to the river as soon as it is light."

And sure enough, there was the carp.

But Charming only gave him two little pats and said nothing, and very soon he fell asleep.

At the first glimmer of dawn Frisk began to jump about, and when he had waked Charming they went out together, first into the garden, and then down to the river's brink, where they wandered up and down. Charming was thinking sadly of having to go back unsuccessful when he heard someone calling: "Charming, Charming!" He looked all about him and thought he must be dreaming, as he could not see anybody. Then he walked on and the voice called again: "Charming, Charming!"

"Who calls me?" said he. Frisk, who was very small and could look closely into the water, cried out: "I see a golden carp coming." And sure enough there was the great carp, who said to Charming:

"You saved my life in the meadow by the willow tree, and I promised that I would repay you. Take this, it is Princess Goldilocks' ring." Charming took the ring out of Dame Carp's mouth, thanking her a thousand times, and he and tiny Frisk went straight to the palace, where someone told the Princess that he was asking to see her.

"Ah! poor fellow," said she, "he must have come to say good-bye, finding it impossible to do as I asked."

So in came Charming, who presented her with the ring and said:

"Madam, I have done your bidding. Will it please you to marry my master?" When the Princess saw her ring brought back to her unhurt she was so astonished that she thought she must be dreaming.

"Truly, Charming," said she, "you must be the favorite of some fairy, or you could never have found it."

"Madam," answered he, "I was helped by nothing but my desire to obey your wishes."

"Since you are so kind," said she, "perhaps you will do me another service, for till it is done I will never be married. There is a prince not far from here whose name is Galifron, who once wanted to marry me, but when I refused he uttered the most terrible threats against me, and vowed that he would lay waste my country. But what could I do? I could not marry a frightful giant as tall as a tower, who eats up people as a monkey eats chestnuts, and who talks so loud that anybody who has to listen to him becomes quite deaf. Nevertheless, he does not cease to persecute me and to kill my subjects. So before I can listen to your proposal you must kill him and bring me his head."

Charming was rather dismayed at this command, but he answered:

"Very well, Princess, I will fight this Galifron; I believe that he will kill me, but at any rate I shall die in your defence."

Then the Princess was frightened and said everything she could think of to prevent Charming from fighting the giant, but it was of no use, and he went out to arm himself suitably, and then, taking little Frisk with him, he mounted his horse and set out for Galifron's country. Everyone he met told him what a terrible giant Galifron was, and that nobody dared go near him; and the more he heard the more frightened he grew. Frisk tried to encourage him by saying:

Before long he saw Galifron coming.

"While you are fighting the giant, dear master, I will go and bite his heels, and when he stoops down to look at me you can kill him."

Charming praised his little dog's plan, but knew that his help would not do much good.

At last he drew near the giant's castle, and saw to his horror that every path that led to it was strewn with bones. Before long he saw Galifron coming. His head was higher than the tallest trees, and he sang in a terrible voice:

> "Bring out your little boys and girls,
> Pray do not stay to do their curls,
> For I shall eat so very many,
> I shall not know if they have any."

Thereupon Charming sang out as loud as he could to the same tune:

> "Come out and meet the valiant Charming,
> Who finds you not at all alarming;
> Although he is not very tall,
> He's big enough to make you fall."

The rhymes were not very correct, but you see he had made them up so quickly that it is a miracle that they were not worse; especially as he was horribly frightened all the time. When Galifron heard these words he looked all about him, and saw Charming standing, sword in hand; this put the giant into a terrible rage, and he aimed a blow at Charming with his huge iron club, which would certainly have killed him if it had reached him, but at that instant a raven perched upon the giant's head, and, pecking with its strong beak and beating with its great wings, so confused and blinded him that all his blows fell harmlessly upon the air, and Charming, rushing in, gave him several strokes with his sharp sword so that he fell to the ground.

Whereupon Charming cut off his head before he knew anything about it, and the raven from a tree close by croaked out:

"You see I have not forgotten the good turn you did me in killing the eagle. To-day I think I have fulfilled my promise of repaying you."

"Indeed, I owe you more gratitude than you ever owed me," replied Charming.

And then he mounted his horse and rode off with Galifron's head.

When he reached the city the people ran after him in crowds, crying:

"Behold the brave Charming, who has killed the giant!" And their shouts reached the Princess's ear, but she dared not ask what was happening, for fear she should hear that Charming had been killed. But very soon he arrived at the palace with the giant's head, of which she was still terrified, though it could no longer do her any harm.

"Princess," said Charming, "I have killed your enemy; I hope you will now consent to marry the King my master."

"Oh dear! no," said the Princess, "not until you have brought me some water from the Gloomy Cavern.

"Not far from here there is a deep cave, the entrance to which is guarded by two dragons with fiery eyes, who will not allow anyone to pass them. When you get into the cavern you will find an immense hole, which you must go down, and it is full of toads and snakes; at the bottom of this hole there is another little cave, in which rises the Fountain of Health and Beauty. It is some of this water that I really must have: everything it touches becomes wonderful. The beautiful things will always remain beautiful, and the ugly things become lovely. If one is young one never grows old, and if one is old one becomes young. You see, Charming, I could not leave my kingdom without taking some of it with me."

"Princess," said he, "you at least can never need this water, but I am an unhappy ambassador, whose death you desire. Where you send me I will go, though I know I shall never return."

And, as the Princess Goldilocks showed no sign of relenting, he started with his little dog for the Gloomy Cavern. Everyone he met on the way said:

"What a pity that a handsome young man should throw away his life so carelessly! He is going to the cavern alone, though if he had a hundred men with him he could not succeed. Why does the Princess ask impossibilities?"

Charming said nothing, but he was very sad. When he was near the top of a hill he dismounted to let his horse graze, while Frisk amused himself by chasing flies. Charming knew he could not be far from the Gloomy Cavern, and on looking about him he saw a black hideous rock from which came a thick smoke, followed in a moment by one of the dragons with fire blazing from his mouth and eyes. His body was yellow and green, and his claws scarlet, and his tail was so long that it lay in a hundred coils. Frisk was so terrified at the sight of it that he did not know where to hide. Charming, quite determined to get the water or die, now drew his sword, and, taking the crystal flask which Pretty Goldilocks had given him to fill, said to Frisk:

"I feel sure that I shall never come back from this expedition; when I am dead, go to the Princess and tell her that her errand has cost me my life. Then find the King my master, and relate all my adventures to him."

As he spoke he heard a voice calling: "Charming, Charming!"

"Who calls me?" said he; then he saw an owl sitting in a hollow tree, who said to him:

"You saved my life when I was caught in the net, now I can repay you. Trust me with the flask, for I know all the ways of the Gloomy Cavern, and can fill it from the Fountain of Beauty." Charming was only too glad to give her the flask, and she flitted into the cavern quite unnoticed by the dragon, and after some time returned with the flask, filled to the very brim with sparkling water. Charming thanked her with all his heart, and joyfully hastened back to the town.

He went straight to the palace and gave the flask to the Princess, who had no further objection to make. So she thanked Charming, and ordered that preparations should be made for her departure, and they soon set out together. The Princess found Charming such an agreeable companion that she sometimes said to him:

"Why didn't we stay where we were? I could have made you king, and we should have been so happy!"

But Charming only answered:

"I could not have done anything that would have vexed my master so much, even for a kingdom, or to please you, though I think you are as beautiful as the sun."

At last they reached the King's great city, and he came out to meet the Princess, bringing magnificent presents, and the marriage was celebrated with great rejoicings. But Goldilocks was so fond of Charming that she could not be happy unless he was near her, and she was always singing his praises.

"If it hadn't been for Charming," she said to the King, "I should never have come here; you ought to be very much obliged to him, for he did the most impossible things and got me water from the Fountain of Beauty, so I can never grow old, and shall get prettier every year."

Little Frisk came to console him.

Then Charming's enemies said to the King:

"It is a wonder that you are not jealous, the Queen thinks there is nobody in the world like Charming. As if anybody you had sent could not have done just as much!"

"It is quite true, now I come to think of it," said the King. "Let him be chained hand and foot, and thrown into the tower."

So they took Charming, and as a reward for having served the King so faithfully he was shut up in the tower, where he only saw the jailer, who brought him a piece of black bread and a pitcher of water every day.

However, little Frisk came to console him, and told him all the news.

When Pretty Goldilocks heard what had happened she threw herself at the King's feet and begged him to set Charming free, but the more she cried the more angry he was, and at last she saw that it was useless to say any more; but it made her very sad. Then the King took it in his head that perhaps he was not handsome enough to please the Princess Goldilocks, and he thought he would bathe his face with the water from the Fountain of Beauty, which was in the flask on a shelf in the Princess's room, where she had placed it that she might see it often. Now it happened that one of the Princess's ladies in chasing a spider had knocked the flask off the shelf and broken it, and every drop of the water had been spilt. Not knowing what to do, she had hastily swept away the pieces of crystal, and then remembered that in the King's room she had seen a flask of exactly the same shape, also filled with sparkling water. So, without saying a word, she fetched it and stood it upon the Queen's shelf.

Now the water in this flask was what was used in the kingdom for getting rid of troublesome people. Instead of having their heads cut off in the usual way, their faces were bathed with the water, and they instantly fell asleep and never woke up any more. So, when the King, thinking to improve his beauty, took the flask and sprinkled the water upon his face, *he* fell asleep, and nobody could wake him.

Little Frisk was the first to hear the news, and he ran to tell Charming, who sent him to beg the Princess not to forget the poor prisoner. All the palace was in confusion on account of the King's death, but tiny Frisk made his way through the crowd to the Princess's side, and said:

"Madam, do not forget poor Charming!"

Then she remembered all he had done for her, and without saying a word to anyone went straight to the tower, and with her own hands took off Charming's chains. Then, putting a golden crown upon his head, and the royal mantle upon his shoulders, she said:

"Come, faithful Charming, I make you king, and will take you for my husband."

Charming, once more free and happy, fell at her feet and thanked her for her gracious words.

Everybody was delighted that he should be king, and the wedding, which took place at once, was the prettiest that can be imagined, and Prince Charming and Princess Goldilocks lived happily ever after.

Snow-white and Rose-red

A POOR WIDOW once lived in a little cottage with a garden in front of it, in which grew two rose trees, one bearing white roses and the other red. She had two children, who were just like the two rose trees; one was called Snow-white and the other Rose-red, and they were the sweetest and best children in the world, always diligent and always cheerful; but Snow-white was quieter and more gentle than Rose-red. Rose-red loved to run about the fields and meadows, and to pick flowers and catch butterflies; but Snow-white sat at home with her mother and helped her in the household, or read aloud to her when there was no work to do. The two children loved each other so dearly that they always walked about hand-in-hand whenever they went out together, and when Snow-white said: "We will never desert each other," Rose-red answered: "No, not as long as we live"; and the mother added: "Whatever one gets she shall share with the other." They often roamed about in the woods gathering berries and no beast offered to hurt them; on the contrary, they came up to them in the most confiding manner; the little hare would eat a cabbage leaf from their hands, the deer grazed beside them, the stag would bound past them merrily, and the birds remained on the branches and sang to them with all their might. No evil ever befell them; if they tarried late in the wood and night overtook them, they lay down together on the moss and slept till morning, and their mother knew they were quite safe, and never felt anxious about them. Once, when they had slept the night in the wood and had been wakened by the morning sun, they perceived a beautiful child in a shining white robe sitting close to their resting-place. The figure got up, looked at them kindly, but said nothing, and vanished into the wood. And when they looked round about them they became aware that they had slept quite close to a precipice, over which they would certainly have fallen had they gone on a few steps further in the darkness. And when they told their mother of their adventure, she said what they had seen must have been the angel that guards good children.

Snow-white and Rose-red kept their mother's cottage so beautifully clean and neat that it was a pleasure to go into it. In summer Rose-red looked after the house, and every morning before her mother awoke she placed a bunch of flowers before the bed, from each tree a rose. In winter Snow-white lit the fire and put on the kettle, which was made of brass, but so beautifully polished that it shone like gold. In the evening when the snowflakes fell their mother said: "Snow-white, go and close the shutters"; and they drew round the fire, while the mother put on her spectacles and read aloud from a big book and the two girls listened and sat and span. Beside them on the ground lay a little lamb, and behind them perched a little white dove with its head tucked under its wings.

One evening as they sat thus cosily together some-one knocked at the door as though he desired admittance. The mother said: "Rose-red, open the door quickly; it must be some traveller seeking shelter." Rose-red hastened to unbar the door, and thought she saw a poor man standing in the darkness outside; but it was no such thing, only a bear, who poked his thick black head through the door. Rose-red screamed aloud and sprang back in terror, the lamb began to bleat, the dove flapped its wings, and Snow-white ran and hid behind her mother's bed. But the bear began to speak, and said: "Don't be afraid: I won't hurt you. I am half frozen, and only wish to warm myself a little." "My poor bear," said the mother, "lie down by the fire, only take care you don't burn your fur." Then she called out:

A bear poked his head through the door.

"Snow-white and Rose-red, come out; the bear will do
you no harm: he is a good, honest creature." So they
both came out of their hiding-places, and gradually the
lamb and dove drew near too, and they all forgot their
fear. The bear asked the children to beat the snow a little out of his fur, and they fetched a brush and
scrubbed him till he was dry. Then the beast stretched
himself in front of the fire, and growled quite happily
and comfortably. The children soon grew quite at their
ease with him, and led their helpless guest a fearful life.
They tugged his fur with their hands, put their small
feet on his back, and rolled him about here and there,
or took a hazel wand and beat him with it; and if he
growled they only laughed. The bear submitted to
everything with the best possible good-nature, only
when they went too far he cried: "Oh! children, spare
my life!

> Snow-white and Rose-red,
> Don't beat your lover dead."

When it was time to retire for the night, and the others went to bed, the mother said to the bear: "You can
lie there on the hearth, in heaven's name; it will be shelter for you from the cold and wet." As soon as day
dawned the children let him out, and he trotted over
the snow into the wood. From this time on the bear
came every evening at the same hour, and lay down by
the hearth and let the children play what pranks they
liked with him; and they got so accustomed to him that
the door was never shut till their black friend had made
his appearance.

When spring came, and all outside was green, the
bear said one morning to Snow-white: "Now I must go
away, and not return again the whole summer." "Where
are you going to, dear bear?" asked Snow-white. "I must

go to the wood and protect my treasure from the wicked dwarfs. In winter, when the earth is frozen hard, they are obliged to remain underground, for they can't work their way through; but now, when the sun has thawed and warmed the ground, they break through and come up above to spy the land and steal what they can: what once falls into their hands and into their caves is not easily brought back to light." Snow-white was quite sad over their friend's departure, and when she unbarred the door for him, the bear, stepping out, caught a piece of his fur in the door-knocker, and Snow-white thought she caught sight of glittering gold beneath it, but she couldn't be certain of it; and the bear ran hastily away, and soon disappeared behind the trees.

A short time after this the mother sent the children into the wood to collect fagots. They came in their wanderings upon a big tree which lay felled on the ground, and on the trunk among the long grass they noticed something jumping up and down, but what it was they couldn't distinguish. When they approached nearer they perceived a dwarf with a wizened face and a beard a yard long. The end of the beard was jammed into a cleft of the tree, and the little man sprang about like a dog on a chain, and didn't seem to know what he was to do. He glared at the girls with his fiery red eyes, and screamed out: "What are you standing there for? can't you come and help me?" "What were you doing, little man?" asked Rose-red. "You stupid, inquisitive goose!" replied the dwarf; "I wanted to split the tree, in order to get little chips of wood for our kitchen fire; those thick logs that serve to make fires for coarse, greedy people like yourselves quite burn up all the little food we need. I had successfully driven in the wedge, and all was going well, but the cursed wood was so slippery that it

The end of his beard was jammed into the tree.

suddenly sprang out, and the tree closed up so rapidly that I had no time to take my beautiful white beard out, so here I am stuck fast, and I can't get away; and you silly, smooth-faced, milk-and-water girls just stand and laugh! Ugh! what wretches you are!"

The children did all in their power, but they couldn't get the beard out; it was wedged in far too firmly. "I will run and fetch somebody," said Rose-red. "Crazy blockheads!" snapped the dwarf; "what's the good of calling anyone else? you're already two too many for me. Does nothing better occur to you than that?" "Don't be so impatient," said Snow-white, "I'll see you get help"; and taking her scissors out of her pocket she cut the end off his beard. As soon as the dwarf felt himself free he seized a bag full of gold which was hidden among the roots of the tree, lifted it up, and muttered aloud:

"Curse these rude wretches, cutting off a piece of my splendid beard!" With these words he swung the bag over his back, and disappeared without as much as looking at the children again.

Shortly after this Snow-white and Rose-red went out to get a dish of fish. As they approached the stream they saw something which looked like an enormous grasshopper, springing towards the water as if it were going to jump in. They ran forward and recognised their old friend the dwarf. "Where are you going to?" asked Rose-red; "you're surely not going to jump into the water?" "I'm not such a fool," screamed the dwarf. "Don't you see that cursed fish is trying to drag me in?" The little man had been sitting on the bank fishing, when unfortunately the wind had entangled his beard

The eagle was about to carry the dwarf off.

in the line; and when immediately afterwards a big fish bit, the feeble little creature had no strength to pull it out; the fish had the upper fin, and dragged the dwarf towards him. He clung on with all his might to every rush and blade of grass, but it didn't help him much; he had to follow every movement of the fish, and was in great danger of being drawn into the water. The girls came up just at the right moment, held him firm, and did all they could to disentangle his beard from the line; but in vain, beard and line were in a hopeless muddle. Nothing remained but to produce the scissors and cut the beard, by which a small part of it was sacrificed.

When the dwarf perceived what they were about he yelled to them: "Do you call that manners, you toadstools! to disfigure a fellow's face? it wasn't enough that you shortened my beard before, but you must now needs cut off the best bit of it. I can't appear like this before my own people. I wish you'd been at Jericho first." Then he fetched a sack of pearls that lay among the rushes, and without saying another word he dragged it away and disappeared behind a stone.

It happened that soon after this the mother sent the two girls to the town to buy needles, thread, laces, and ribbons. Their road led over a heath where huge boulders of rock lay scattered here and there. While trudging along they saw a big bird hovering in the air, circling slowly above them, but always descending lower, till at last it settled on a rock not far from them. Immediately afterwards they heard a sharp, piercing cry. They ran forward, and saw with horror that the eagle had pounced on their old friend the dwarf, and was about to carry him off. The tender-hearted children seized a hold of the little man, and struggled so long with the bird that at last he let go his prey. When the dwarf had recovered from the first shock he screamed in his screeching voice: "Couldn't you have treated me more carefully? you have torn my thin little coat all to shreds, useless, awkward hussies that you are!" Then he took a bag of precious stones and vanished under the rocks into his cave. The girls were accustomed to his ingratitude, and went on their way and did their business in town. On their way home, as they were again passing the heath, they surprised the dwarf pouring out his precious stones on an open space, for he had thought no one would pass by at so late an hour. The evening sun shone on the glittering stones, and they glanced and gleamed so beautifully that the children stood still and gazed on them. "What are you standing there gaping for?" screamed the dwarf, and his ashen-grey face became scarlet with rage. He was about to go off with these angry words when a sudden growl was heard, and a black bear trotted out of the wood. The dwarf jumped up in a great fright, but he hadn't time to reach his place of retreat, for the bear was already close to him. Then he cried in terror: "Dear Mr. Bear, spare me! I'll give you all my treasure. Look at those beautiful precious stones lying there. Spare my life! what pleasure would you get from a poor feeble little fellow like me? You won't feel me between your teeth. There, lay hold of these two wicked girls, they will be a tender morsel for you, as fat as young quails; eat them up, for heaven's sake." But the bear, paying no attention to his words, gave the evil little creature one blow with his paw, and he never moved again.

The girls had run away, but the bear called after them: "Snow-white and Rose-red, don't be afraid; wait, and I'll come with you." Then they recognised his voice and stood still, and when the bear was quite close to them his skin suddenly fell off, and a beautiful man stood beside them, all dressed in gold. "I am a king's son," he said, "and have been doomed by that unholy little dwarf, who had stolen my treasure, to roam about the woods as a wild bear till his death should set me free. Now he has got his well-merited punishment."

Snow-white married him, and Rose-red his brother, and they divided the great treasure the dwarf had collected in his cave between them. The old mother lived for many years peacefully with her children; and she carried the two rose trees with her, and they stood in front of her window, and every year they bore the finest red and white roses.